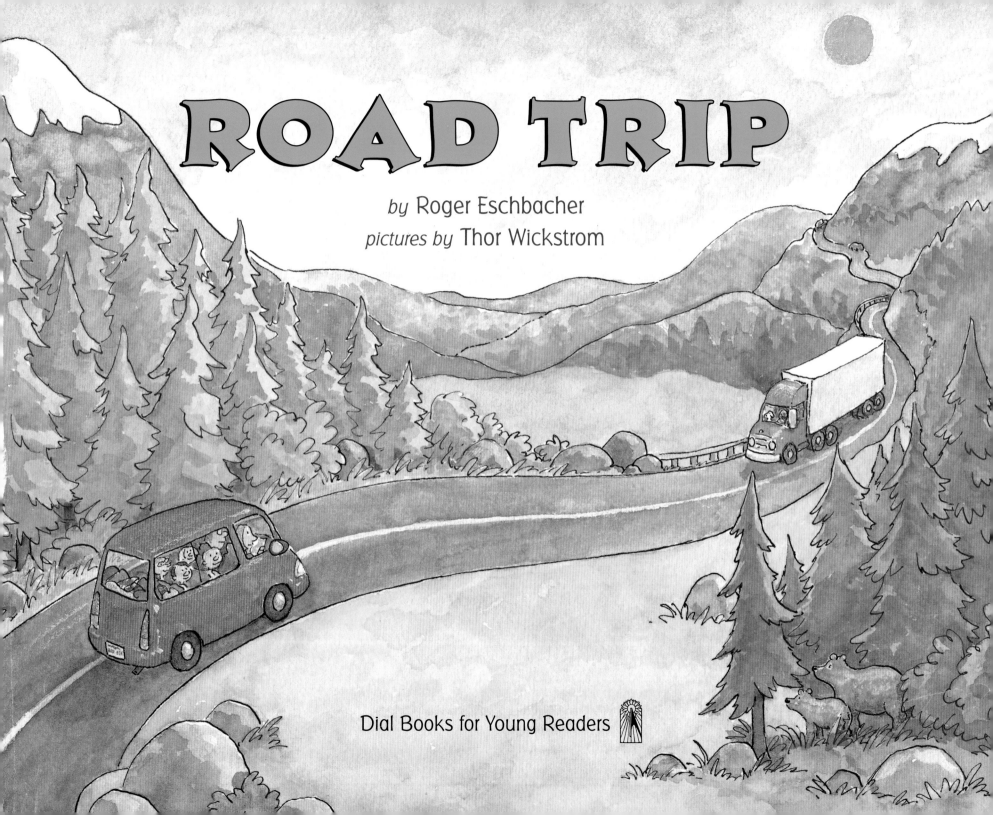

ROAD TRIP

by Roger Eschbacher

pictures by Thor Wickstrom

Dial Books for Young Readers

DIAL BOOKS FOR YOUNG READERS
A division of Penguin Young Readers Group
Published by The Penguin Group
Penguin Group (USA) Inc., 375 Hudson Street, New York, NY 10014, U.S.A.
Penguin Group (Canada), 90 Eglinton Avenue East, Suite 700, Toronto, Ontario, Canada M4P 2Y3
(a division of Pearson Penguin Canada Inc.)
Penguin Books Ltd, 80 Strand, London WC2R 0RL, England
Penguin Ireland, 25 St. Stephen's Green, Dublin 2, Ireland (a division of Penguin Books Ltd.)
Penguin Group (Australia), 250 Camberwell Road, Camberwell Victoria 3124, Australia
(a division of Pearson Australia Group Pty Ltd)
Penguin Books India Pvt Ltd, 11 Community Centre, Panchsheel Park, New Delhi - 110 017, India.
Penguin Group (NZ), Cnr Airborne and Rosedale Roads, Albany, Auckland 1310, New Zealand
(a division of Pearson New Zealand Ltd)
Penguin Books (South Africa) (Pty) Ltd, 24 Sturdee Avenue, Rosebank, Johannesburg 2196, South Africa.
Penguin Books Ltd, Registered Offices: 80 Strand, London WC2R 0RL, England

Designed by Jasmin Rubero
Text set in Badger Light
Manufactured in China on acid-free paper
The publisher does not have any control over and does not assume any
responsibility for author or third-party websites or their content.

10 9 8 7 6 5 4 3 2 1

Library of Congress Cataloging-in-Publication Data
Eschbacher, Roger.
Road trip / by Roger Eschbacher ; pictures by Thor Wickstrom.
p.   cm.
Summary: A family piles into their car to head for a family reunion, embarking on a road trip that includes
songs, games, food, roadside attractions, and motels.
ISBN 0-8037-2927-8
[1. Automobile travel—Fiction. 2. Family reunions—Fiction. 3. Family life—Fiction.
4. Stories in rhyme.] 1. Wickstrom, Thor, ill. 11. Title.
PZ8.3.E84Ro 2006
[E]—dc22
2004015309

*The art was created using ink and watercolor
on paper with color pencil*

To my parents, Pat and Roger, who taught me
to love the spaces between places
—R.E.

To my family—Bernie, Darlene, Valerie,
Karl, and Sosha, with fond
memories of our marathon road trips
—T.W.

Wake Up!

Early morning,
Alarm clocks warning.
Pile into the family car.

Sisters, brother,
Father, Mother—
Time to go, we're driving far!

Our vacation
Destination:
Grandma's house, two days away.
Across the nation
To that location,
Food and fun along the way!

First Stop

Fill the tank with gasoline.
Pick the pump marked unleaded.
Wash the windows, squeaky-clean.
The open road is where we're headed!

Maps

North, south, east, west,
No matter how you hold it,
A map can put you to the test,
When you try to fold it.

Road Warriors

"Mom! Mom! She's looking at me!"
"Dad! Dad! He's poking my knee!"
"All right, you kids, don't make a sound,
Or else I'll turn this car around!"

So we're quiet until...

Sing Along

"The ants go marching one by one," my mother starts to sing.
Each of us joins in at once—singing is our thing!
When ant one hundred comes along,
We're desperate for another song.
So when Mom starts "The Hokey Pokey"—
We think that's just okey-dokey!

I Spy

I Spy with my little eye,
A secret something passing by.
It's in that field inside those fences.
A drink is what this "thing" dispenses.

I Spy with my little eye,
A *mooing* something passing by.
It's black and white; its hide is dotted.
Can you guess what I just spotted?

Squish!

Grasshoppers have greenish guts.
Beetles are more brownish.
Katydids are smashed up nuts.
Butterflies are clownish.

A final clash of wings and gas
Is a fate no creature chooses.
For in the fight between bug and glass,
An insect always loses!

License Plate Bingo

A, B, C, D, E, F, G,
How many letters can you see?
H, I, J, K, L, M, N, O, P,
Why oh why can't I find Z?!

Q, R, S—my brother's got them.
T, U, V—it's hard to spot them!
W, X, Y—Yahoo! My letter!
AriZona's never looked better!

Road Food

"Look for trucks!" my father said.
"That's where you'll get great meals.
A trucker likes to be well fed,
When driving eighteen wheels."

At Diesel Danny's Sandwich Shed,
Our waitress is named Ruth.
Her giant hair is fiery red,
Just like our giant booth.

Fried steak, milk shake, apple pie,
Coffee thick as gravy,
Hominy, grits, ham on rye,
The Jell-O's green and wavy!

Too much food! Gone too far!
Feeling really bloated.
Slowly stumbling to the car,
Belly fully loaded.

And soon . . .

Gotta Go!

Gotta go, go, go!
Can we stop, stop, stop?
Dad says no, no, no!
Will I pop, pop, pop?!

Cornfields

Cornfields, cornfields, boring cornfields,
As far as I can see.
Cornfields, cornfields, snoring cornfields—
Why don't they plant a tree?

Forests!

Forests, forests, boring forests,
I'm feeling tired and worn.
Forests, forests, snoring forests,
Now I miss the corn.

Motel

There it is just up ahead,
A neon light oasis.
A room, a pool, some ice, some beds,
Just waiting to embrace us.

Dad checks us in, Mom checks the place
To make sure that it's clean.
We kids pile out and run a race
Down to the snack machine!

I crawl in bed and shut my eyes—
Four hundred miles today!
We'll snooze a bit before we rise,
And then—we're on our way!

Attractions

Caverns, Sink Holes, Mystery Spots,
Balls of String and Giant Knots.
We pull off at Exit Five,
And go to visit Bunyan's Hive.

Bunyan's Hive is quite astounding.
Giant bees and wax abounding.
Buy some candy made from honey.
Queen Bee gladly takes our money.

Gulp some soda, climb the comb,
Take a tour with Drone Jerome.
Bunyan's Hive has lots to see.
Visit the "Home of the Giant Bee"!

Postcards

At every stop along the way,
We buy a lot of cards.
We write 'em up and mail 'em home,
Complete with our regards.

Each postcard shows a local spot:
"Come see our Haunted Cantaloupe!"
Check out this one I just bought—
A Southern Crested Jackalope?!

POSTCARDS
3 FOR $1.00

Greetings from The World Famous HAUNTED CANTALOUPE!

Gone Fishin'... VIKING LAKE!

Yup, it's a Southern Crested Jackalope!

Are We There Yet?

Are we there yet?
Are we there yet?
Are we there yet?
We moan.

No we're not yet!
No we're not yet!
No we're not yet!
They groan.

Reunion

Grandma! Grandpa! Hugging time!
Everybody's here!
Grandpa Joseph found a dime
Tucked behind my ear!

to the
REUNION!

Burgers, hot dogs, soda, chips,
Baked beans by the ton,
Coleslaw, pickles, onion dips
—Don't forget the bun!

Family Tree

A reunion is a celebration
We wouldn't want to miss.
We've traveled clear across our nation
For a chance to reminisce.

And even though we're all spread out
From sea to shining sea,
We gather now to dance about
Our good old family tree.

Driving Back

Load the car up with a sigh.
Climb inside, then say good-bye.
What's bad about a trip by car?

The drive back home seems twice as far.

We're Home at Last!

We're home at last, let's all unpack,
And put away our things—
Souvenirs for looking back,
For fond rememberings.

We're home at last, I hear a tap,
My friends come through the door.
About my trip I start to yap,
Can't wait to tell them more!

We're home at last, I wonder where
We'll go next time we load
The family car and then declare:

"Let's hit the open road!"